One Snowy Day

Tracey Corderoy

Illustrated by Hannah Whitty

SCHOLASTIC

First published in the UK in 2012 by Scholastic Children's Books
An imprint of Scholastic Ltd
Euston House, 24 Eversholt Street
London, NW1 1DB, UK
Registered office: Westfield Road, Southam, Warwickshire, CV47 0RA
SCHOLASTIC and associated logos are trademarks and/
or registered trademarks of Scholastic Inc.

ISBN 978 1 407 13483 3

A CIP catalogue record for this book
is available from the British Library.

Printed and bound by CPI Group (UK) Ltd, Croydon, CR0 4YY
Papers used by Scholastic Children's Books
are made from wood grown in sustainable forests.

1 3 5 7 9 10 8 6 4 2

www.scholastic.co.uk/zone
www.traceycorderoy.com

For Mark, for all your love and support. . .

T.C xx

WILLOW VALLEY

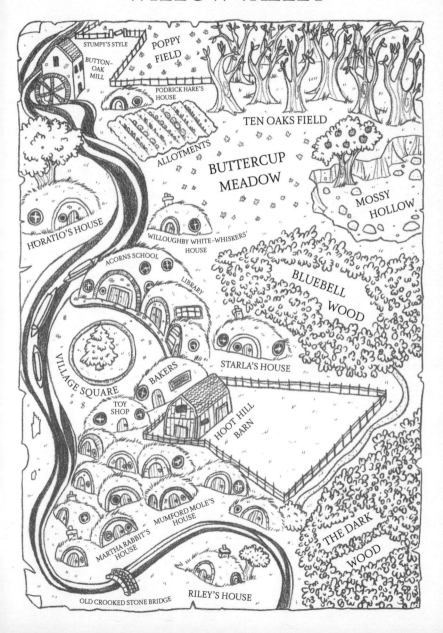

Chapter 1

It was Christmas time in Willow Valley and the air buzzed with excitement. Curls of white smoke danced from the chimneys of the cave-houses dotted on the hills, as the animals huddled around crackling fires writing Christmas cards or making pretty decorations.

Willow Valley was a special place at any time of year. It was surrounded by rolling green hills, dotted with trees and flowers. There were daffodils and primroses in the spring, poppies and cornflowers in the summer.

In the autumn, the bushes were loaded with blackberries, big and juicy and purple! And in the wintertime, as it was now, holly with berries as red as apples lined the banks of the river, and the bare trees were iced with sparkling frost.

In one of the cave-houses, Riley, a little toffee-coloured mouse, was kneeling on the rug in his kitchen. Beside him were his two best friends – Starla, a little fluffy badger, and a roly-poly hedgehog called Horatio Spark.

Riley, Horatio and Starla had been

friends since they were babies even though they were all very different.

Riley was the one who most loved adventures. When he grew up he wanted to be an explorer. Starla was sensible, thoughtful and kind. She liked reading and giggling at the boys when they had crazy ideas. And nobody had crazier ideas than *Horatio*.

Horatio always seemed to get into mischief though he never meant any harm. He just liked to "do" things. These were usually silly things, and Horatio never thought before he did them!

Today the three friends were making

Christmas decorations as they were getting their Christmas trees tomorrow. Everyone was so excited as they beavered away!

Riley loved reindeers so he was wearing special Christmas antlers. He held up a paper chain he'd been cutting out. "Look!" he smiled, as a long row of reindeers dangled down.

Each one had the top of their left antler missing where his scissors had accidentally slipped. But Riley didn't care. No one would notice when they were hanging on his tree!

Starla looked at the reindeers and smiled. "And look at my twinkle-cones!" she said. She picked up a fir cone she'd been painting gold and sprinkled it with silver glitter.

"There!" she beamed, and she popped it down beside a pile she'd just glittered. "Now I just need to tie on the sparkly ribbon. Then they're all done."

"I'm nearly finished, too!" cried Horatio.

He'd been making a huge star out of newspaper and gloopy glue.

"I'll paint it later," he said. "It's going to sit at the top of my Christmas tree!"

"You'll have to get a really big tree then," grinned Starla. Horatio's star was enormous.

Just then, Riley's little sister skipped over. "Look at this!" squeaked Mimi-Rose. She held out a robin she had made from brown wool, felt and bendy pipe cleaners. "And Mummy's mince pies smell like they're ready too!"

Everyone looked across as Riley's mum

took the pies from the oven. "Mmm," said Riley, as the smell of spiced fruit wafted under his nose. His whiskers quivered excitedly. *This* was the smell of Christmas!

They crowded round the table and watched, open mouthed, as Riley's mum popped the freshly cooked pies on to a rack to cool. Now they just needed to be dusted with icing sugar.

Riley's mum shook a small sieve over the pies and the icing sugar tumbled through like snowflakes.

"Wheee!" giggled Mimi-Rose. "It looks just like it's snowing!"

Riley and his friends gazed longingly at the pies. "Mmmm. . ." breathed Horatio, licking his lips. "After ginger cake, you know, mince pies are my *favourite* things!"

Riley's mum smiled. "So who'd like to try one?"

"Me!" cried everyone, waving their paws.

They dived on to chairs and eagerly waited as plates were brought from the big dresser. Then Riley's mum took out a full jug of cream from the fridge.

The mince pies were served and they all tucked in. *"Yum!"* said Riley, as big blobs of cream sat on his whiskers like snowballs.

"It's snowed on Riley too!" giggled Mimi-Rose.

How Riley wished it would *really* snow! The sky had been steely grey for days but not a single snowflake had fallen. Willow Valley, with its rolling hills, was the perfect place for sledging!

"Mum," said Riley, "do you think it *will* snow?"

"Well, it's certainly cold enough!" replied his mum.

"Lucky we've got mince pies to warm us up!" beamed Horatio.

Just as they had all finished eating, Starla's grandfather, Willoughby

White-Whiskers, appeared to take her and Horatio home. "Are you ready for our trip tomorrow?" he asked.

"I am!" cried Riley.

"Me too!" Starla smiled.

"Me three!" boomed Horatio brightly.

This year Starla's grandfather was taking them to choose their Christmas trees from Dingle Wood. It would be extra exciting because they would be sailing there in a narrowboat!

The Willow Valley animals had three narrowboats called the *Whirligig*, the *Dragonfly* and the *Kingfisher*.

The *Whirligig* was the biggest boat. It was dark blue in colour with small pink roses and little beetles painted around its windows. The *Dragonfly* was smaller and bottle green with a bright red door.

Riley's favourite boat though, was the

Kingfisher. This boat was the colour of a summer sky with a kingfisher painted on its bow. Riley hoped he'd own a boat like this when he was a famous explorer!

The narrowboats were mostly used for market trips when everyone would sail out of Willow Valley to sell the goods they'd made. These trips were now over until the spring, so Willoughby, who was the captain of the fleet, had decided to use the *Kingfisher* to go on their Christmas tree adventure. Everyone knew that the best Christmas trees were to be found in Dingle Wood, but the friends couldn't wait much longer to get theirs.

Christmas Day was only *three* sleeps away!

Starla and Horatio put on their scarves and gathered up their decorations. Horatio borrowed a tin of gold paint too as he planned to finish his star after supper that night.

"We're ready, Grandpa!" Starla smiled.

"Off we go then!" said Willoughby.

He opened the door and led them out into the chilly night. The indigo sky was dotted with stars, and candles flickered in cave-house windows, like little lighthouses guiding the way back home.

Riley waved his friends off from the cave-house door. As he did, he spotted something small and white floating down through the sky.

"A snowflake!" he cried, and he leapt up and caught it. But it wasn't wet and it wasn't cold and it didn't melt in his warm, fluffy paw.

"Oh," Riley grumbled. It was only a feather!

Riley blew the feather back into the sky then hurried inside where supper was now waiting on the table. His mum had cooked a big parsnip pie with thick, golden pastry. "Yum!" said Riley, grabbing his fork. He was starving!

As they ate, they talked about the Christmas tree that Riley would choose tomorrow. His dad, Barty Black-Paw, always used to choose their tree. But then, one night, he had gone exploring in The Dark Wood and, sadly, he had never returned. . .

Now choosing the tree would be Riley's job. What an important job it was too!

"It mustn't be too small," Mimi-Rose said. "Or too big. Or too wonky!"

She told him about the story of Goldilocks where everything had to be *"just right"* or it was simply all wrong.

"All wrong!" gulped Riley, his eyes growing wide. What if the tree he chose was all wrong too?

"It'll be OK," whispered his mum. "I know you'll do a great job." She winked and Riley gave a small smile back.

"Thanks, Mum."

They finished their supper and Riley hurried to bed. He was setting off very early in the morning and he didn't want to be tired.

Riley washed, cleaned his teeth and pulled on his nightcap super, super fast! Then he dived into his freezing cold bed.

"Brrrr!" he shivered from deep under his blankets. "Night night!"

Chapter 2

The next morning when Riley's mum woke him it was still dark. She tapped his little fluffy paw. "Riley," she whispered. "Time to get up."

Riley's nose wrinkled up as he yawned widely. "Is it time to get our tree?" he asked.

"Yes," his mum replied. "Today's the day."

She lit his lantern with the candle from hers. "I'll go and get your breakfast ready," she said, "while you have a quick wash."

"OK," said Riley, as she pattered off downstairs.

Riley wriggled out of his warm, wool blankets and washed in the chilly bathroom. Two minutes later he appeared in the kitchen, still yawning.

His mum had lit a crackling fire and her big black porridge pot was already on the stove. She gave him some bread and hazelnuts to nibble while his porridge cooked. "What about Mimi-Rose?" asked Riley. His sister was still in bed.

"Don't worry," his mum smiled. "I'll make her porridge later."

After breakfast Riley felt much more awake. He packed his rucksack with mince pies and hung his binoculars around his neck. Now he was ready to go!

"Don't forget your scarf," his mum reminded him. It was going to be another chilly day. She wrapped it around him, and handed him a flask of spiced ginger cordial. "This will keep you warm!"

Suddenly there was a knock at the door, so Riley dashed over and opened it. There on the doorstep stood Mr White-Whiskers with Starla and Horatio. "Ready to go?" Willoughby asked.

"Ready!" Riley nodded and pattered out.

"Have fun!" called his mum from the doorstep as they set off down the path.

"We will!" everyone called back brightly.

The friends walked downhill towards the narrowboats. The grass was hard and crunchy and their warm breath fogged the air. Horatio's cheeks were as bright as berries and Starla was wearing her fluffy pink ear muffs and extra chunky mittens.

Riley shivered, as much from feeling excited as from the cold. Tomorrow was Christmas Eve! By the end of the day he'd have his Christmas tree too!

At the foot of the hill was a trickling river. The *Kingfisher* stood on the cold, clear water, gleaming and ready to go.

Everyone walked carefully up the gangplank as it was quite icy today. "We don't want to fall in the water!" Starla nodded.

When they were all safely on deck, Mr White-Whiskers started the engine and the boat began to purr like a cat. A moment later, they were gliding away. *"Hooray!"* cheered everyone.

As they tootled out of Willow Valley they passed some cave-houses on the hills. A few friends had promised they'd get up early to see them off.

"Hey, there's Bramble!" Horatio cried, as a bleary-eyed bunny waved from his window.

"And look, there's Posy Vole in her spotty pyjamas!"

They sailed on past some willow trees lining the riverbank, and then they saw the big village square. In the middle of

it stood a huge Christmas tree. It was
decorated with lots of little red candles
and colourful baubles and candy canes.
And at its very top sat a pretty gold star.

Bright moonbeams shining down from the sky made the star twinkle and glow. "*My* star's going to look like that," grinned Horatio. "Only bigger!"

Tomorrow night everyone would gather in the village square. All the shops would stay open late and an orchestra of moles would play everyone's favourite Christmas carols!

After the carols all the little ones would nibble roast chestnuts around a crackling bonfire, talking excitedly of what Santa might bring them. Then, when Christmas Day finally came, they would rush around to see their friends and show off their lovely new presents!

As the *Kingfisher* sailed
on, the hills became softer, like rippling
waves. Riley peered through his
binoculars and saw big, square fields
for miles around.

Some were a dark holly-green colour
while others were bright leafy shades.
And a few were a rich chocolate-brown.
These fields all joined together like Starla's
patchwork quilt. Riley imagined an army
of squirrels busily stitching it up. The
journey to Dingle Wood was full of things
to see!

The *Kingfisher* reached Dingle Creek around lunchtime. On one side of the river was a big, open meadow and on the other side stood Dingle Wood.

When the Willow Valley animals came here on their market trips it usually took much longer because then there were so many of them on board. Luckily the *Kingfisher* was lighter today so the journey had gone a lot quicker.

Willoughby White-Whiskers tied up the narrowboat. Then they ate their lunch down below deck huddled round the toasty woodburner. Willoughby had brought flasks of pumpkin soup and crusty bread and cheese. Then, as a very special treat, they all had jam roly-poly and custard for pudding!

When they had finished Willoughby put on his scarf. "Time to choose our trees!" he smiled.

"Yippee!" cheered everyone.

They wrapped up warm and hurried on deck and down the icy gangplank. Dingle Creek looked more magical than ever!

The grass was covered in a dusting of frost which glimmered in the weak winter sunlight, and happy little robins whistled out carols from the fir trees.

The trickling creek had stepping stones, which they carefully crossed. "This way to Dingle Wood!" Willoughby nodded.

He led them into the big dark wood on the other side of the stream. "Now keep your eyes open for the beavers!"

"The beavers?" said Starla. "But . . . why are there *beavers*?"

"You'll see!" her grandfather chuckled. "You'll see!"

They crunched along a hard mud track weaving through the giant fir trees. The wood got thicker and thicker the further in they went.

Suddenly, Horatio stopped in his tracks.

"Wait! What's that noise?" he said. It sounded like *nibbling* to him.

"Ahhh!" Mr White-Whiskers grinned. "The beavers must be very close!"

Horatio sniffed the air hopefully. "But what are they *eating*?" he said. "Do you think they might be having a Christmas party?"

"They're not eating anything!" Willoughby laughed and Horatio's prickles drooped. "Beavers have very long teeth you know, and they use them to nibble down Christmas trees!"

"Oh!" cried Starla. "Then we can *buy* them!"

"Exactly!" replied her grandfather. "Just follow me."

They carried on walking and as they did, the nibbling got louder and louder. Finally, Riley squeaked, "Look! I think we're there!"

Before them stood a little clearing where beavers were selling freshly nibbled-down trees to crowds of excited animals.

Three tiny hedgehogs were playing catch-the-fir-cones as their parents paid for their tree. And, here and there, little badgers and rabbits were skipping beside their mums and dads who were carrying their trees back home.

As they watched, a beaver bounded up. He was wearing a stripey red and green hat which looked like Riley's night cap! On the tip of it was a golden bell which tinkled each time he moved.

"I'm Teasel!" said the beaver, nodding his head. *Ting-a-ling-ling* went the bell! "Here to choose a Christmas tree, are you?" he smiled.

"*Three* trees, actually!" Willoughby replied.

"Ah ha!" said the beaver, with a big toothy grin, nodding his head again. *Ting-a-ling-ling* went the golden bell.

"To the *nibblers* then!" he cried.
"Follow me!"

He led them down a narrow path.
Along each side were high willow
fences, so it felt like being in a maze!

"Isn't this fun?" Riley giggled, feeling
just like an explorer.

"Really fun!" cried Starla and Horatio,
as they followed the beaver and his
tinkling hat.

At last they reached two big stone plant
pots at the end of the narrow pathway.
In each stood a pretty Christmas tree
decorated with ribbons and gingerbread
stars. "Oooh!" squealed Starla. She'd never

seen anything so lovely! And it gave her lots more ideas of how to decorate *her* tree when she got back home.

In the trees' neat branches were tiny fairy lights which looked like *real* fairies. "Fireflies!" cried Riley.

"Eeek!" gulped Horatio. "But their *bottoms* are on fire – look!"

"No they're not!" Starla smiled. "It just *looks* like that! Fireflies' bottoms always glow."

The fireflies were fast asleep now for they liked to play at night. Each time they snored the tips of their tails lit up very brightly. Riley wished *his* Christmas tree could have fireflies too. Mimi-Rose loved anything that twinkled!

Teasel led them out between the pretty Christmas trees. "This is where the nibblers work!" he said. "They need to be in a special fenced-off place because of all the falling trees!"

"Wow!" said Horatio, gazing around. "This is great!"

A team of beavers were gnawing at tree trunks as animals stood a safe way off, eagerly waiting for their Christmas trees to fall.

"The nibblers are busy today," Teasel nodded, his golden bell jingling again.

"*I* want to be a nibbler when I grow up!" Horatio said with a grin. "But I think I'd rather be a *ginger cake* nibbler!"

Teasel led them to a patch of trees. "Which ones would you like?" he asked.

"Could we just have a closer look?" said Willoughby.

"Why, of course!" smiled Teasel. "There are lots to see."

The friends wandered around looking at the trees until they picked out the ones they liked best. Riley chose one – not too big, or too small, and with nice bushy branches. Starla chose one that was very straight and neat.

Horatio's tree was both big *and* bushy
(and a little bit wonky too!). "It has to be
big to hold my star on top!" he boasted.

When their trees had been nibbled
down, Teasel gave them three tiny ones

to plant in their place. "Then *they'll* grow big and strong one day!" he said.

He handed them each a little spade and they planted their trees in a row. When they'd been watered, Teasel called for some carriers. "What are *carriers?*" Horatio asked.

"Beavers who help carry the trees!" Teasel nodded.

With that, three beefy beavers appeared. They scooped the three Christmas trees on to their shoulders then carried them down to the tills, where Willoughby paid for each one.

"Now the carriers will take them back to your boat!" Teasel said brightly.

"Oh, how kind!" Willoughby smiled. "Thank you!"

They said goodbye to Teasel and set off back to the *Kingfisher*. But they hadn't gone far, when Horatio suddenly stopped.

"Hey, was that a *snowflake?*" he said. "Something just whizzed past my nose!"

"It was probably just some sawdust," said Starla.

"Yeah, from the nibblers," Riley added. There was an awful lot of sawdust around.

They carried on walking. The ground was cold and the chilly air stung their ears. Finally, they reached the edge of the wood and stepped out into the daylight. *"Whoa!"* gasped Horatio, pointing a paw. *"Look!"*

The fields and meadows all around were carpeted in soft, white snow and pretty snowflakes were floating down through the sky.

Inside Dingle Wood the thick, bushy trees had been like a big umbrella and had kept the snow as a lovely surprise.

"Yippee!" cheered Riley, leaping into the air. *"It's snowing!"*

Chapter 3

Riley raced around in excited little circles as snowflakes danced down from the sky. Great big ones! White and fluffy and cotton-wool soft!

The snow made the meadow look like a giant marshmallow and small piles of it sat on the robins' heads, as if they were wearing fluffy white bobble hats!

"Oh, Grandpa!" cried Starla. "Can we go and play?"

"Please, Mr White-Whiskers!" begged Riley and Horatio. They had waited all year to have fun in the snow and now it was finally here!

Willoughby White-Whiskers thought for a moment. "Well, we do need to be heading home quite soon, but while I help load the trees on the boat you can go and have a little play."

"Hooray!" cheered everyone, racing across to the meadow.

"Let's throw snowballs!" Starla cried, as snowflakes tumbled down around them.

She scooped up a great big pile of snow and tossed it through the air,

just as Horatio went leaping by. . .
SPLAT!

Starla's snowball hit Horatio's back
and exploded on his prickles. "Hey!"
he chuckled, tossing one too, which
landed – *smack* – on Riley's nose.

"Hee hee!" giggled Riley. "Let's make a *giant* snowball!"

He scooped up some snow, patted it into a ball then started to roll it along the ground. As he did, his snowball grew bigger and bigger!

When it was the size of a cannonball, he pushed it up a snowy bank then sent it tumbling back down. "Catch it!" cried Riley, as his snowball rolled off around the snowy meadow.

"I'll get it!" yelled Horatio. He rolled after it with Starla and Riley racing behind him.

"I *love* snow!" cried Riley.

"Me too!" nodded Starla. *"So much!"*

The snowball trundled here and there with Horatio rolling after it. Nobody could catch it though. It was going so fast!

Then suddenly Riley stopped in his tracks. "Oh no!" he cried. "My snowball! *Look* – it's about to crash into that tree!"

"So is *Horatio*," Starla gasped. "STOP!"

It was too late. The snowball hit the tree and exploded everywhere. Horatio, who was right behind, was buried in a mountain of freezing snow.

"Help!" cried the shivery mountain. *"Get me out of here!"*

Starla and Riley began scooping off
the snow. Then Willoughby ran up and
helped too.

In no time at all, they had dug Horatio
out but he looked very sorry for himself.

"Silly old snowball!" he shivered. "Aaa-*chooo!*"

Willoughby checked him over. "No harm done!" he said. "Right, one last game then we need to go."

"Let's build a snowcastle!" Riley cried. "And a dragon that puffs snow-fire!"

"*Yeah,*" gasped Horatio.

"Good idea!" smiled Starla. "Come on!"

Just then a group of little moles and beavers came racing into the meadow. They were wearing thick scarves and bobble hats and their cheeks were rosy-red. "Come and sledge with us!" called a little mole.

"Oh, can we, Grandpa?" Starla asked.

"Go on then," smiled Willoughby. "But do be careful. Especially you, Horatio!"

"I'm *always* careful," Horatio beamed.

The friends helped the beavers and moles set up a bob sleigh track. Then they took it in turns to whoosh along it on sledges.

One of the moles had a wristwatch and was timing everyone's lap. Riley was the fastest, closely followed by a little beaver. Poor Horatio came last because he kept on trying to do fancy stunts and crashing.

While they'd been sledging, Willoughby had gone back to the *Kingfisher* and made hot chocolate for everyone. "This will warm us all up!" he said.

"Thanks!" the little animals cried. They sat on snowy tree stumps, sipping their steaming mugs of chocolate.

"I'm going to remember this day," smiled Riley. "Always. . ."

"Right!" Willoughby said, as he collected the mugs. "Now we must go home."

"*Oh*," groaned Starla, and Riley's tail drooped.

"Do we *have* to, Mr White-Whiskers?" Horatio asked.

"Yes," nodded Willoughby. "I'm afraid we really do."

He explained that he'd told their parents in Willow Valley that he'd get them back home in time for supper. "We've got quite a long journey ahead," he said.

"OK," sighed Starla, Riley and Horatio together.

They said goodbye to their new friends and climbed aboard the *Kingfisher*. Then Mr White-Whiskers started the engine and they waved as the boat glided off.

"I've had such fun," Starla said.

"It's not over yet!" beamed Riley.

"It's very nearly Christmas!" cried Horatio.

As the boat sailed out of Dingle Creek the snow began to get heavier. It happened quite suddenly – great feathery flakes started tumbling down from the sky. It was as if the clouds were having a pillow fight!

Down below deck Riley and his friends shared the mince pies and spiced cordial he'd brought. Then Riley took some up on a tray for Willoughby.

"Here you are, Mr White-Whiskers," he said. But the wise, old badger looked suddenly worried and the boat felt juddery and slow.

"What's the matter?" Riley asked as Starla and Horatio appeared.

"Hmmm," said Willoughby, scratching his head. "The boat just doesn't feel right. . ."

With that, they heard a crunching noise and the *Kingfisher* came to a stop. "What *is* it, Grandpa?" Starla asked.

Willoughby hurried to the side of the boat and peered into the water. "The river has frozen solid!" he said.

It looked like they were stuck.

Chapter 4

"Oh no!" gasped Starla.

"Eeek!" squeaked Riley.

"I hate getting stuck," groaned Horatio.

Horatio was *always* getting stuck! Once he'd been stuck in a flower pot and once up an old apple tree. It had taken nearly all day to get him down! But he'd never been stuck on a river before. And never *so* stuck that he might miss Christmas. All those presents . . . and fun . . . and *food*!

"Don't worry," said Starla. "Grandpa's clever! He'll get us home, won't you, Grandpa?"

Willoughby smiled as three worried faces peered at him through the snow. "Of course! Now don't you worry," he said. "Come with me. . ."

He led the way back down below deck where the woodburner crackled brightly. "Why not do some drawing?" he said.

"But we want to help you, Mr White-Whiskers," said Riley.

"I know," nodded Willoughby. "And you can! But first I need to work out what to do."

He found them some paper and colouring pencils. "I won't be long," he told them, as he hurried back to check the ice. "You stay here and keep warm," he called behind him.

Everyone was quiet. Even Horatio, who was hardly ever quiet at all. As Riley started drawing, he couldn't help thinking how worried his mum and Mimi-Rose would be if they didn't get back that night.

They might think that, like his dad, Riley might never come home again. And once, when Mimi-Rose had gone missing, his mum had been beside herself with worry!

"Well, *I've* just written a letter!" said Horatio, puffing out his chest importantly.

"Who to?" asked Riley.

"Santa!" said Horatio. And they listened as he read it out. . .

Dear Santa,
I've been very good this year
and these are the things I've been
good at:
1. Brushing my teeth nearly every
   day
2. Not windy-popping (much)
3. Almost sharing my ginger cake
   - three whole times!

So I'm writing to ask if me and my friends could have one little early Christmas present?

Please could you, somehow, get us back home because tomorrow we need to decorate our trees.

Lots of love,

from,

Horatio Spark x x x

"That's a very good letter," Starla said. "But how will Santa get it?"

"Err," said Horatio, scratching his head. "Um . . . ah. . ."

"We could put it in a bottle," Riley suggested, "and send it off down the river? Messages in bottles *always* get where they're meant to."

"Exactly!" cried Horatio. "I was *just* about to say that! Let's do it now, come on!"

So Starla found an empty lemonade bottle and Horatio popped in his rolled-up

letter. Finally, Riley stuffed the cork
in tightly.

Horatio held the bottle as they
hurried on deck. Willoughby turned
and told them he'd thought of a plan
to get them home safely. Riley should
have known he'd come up with
something. Willoughby was the
captain of the Willow Valley fleet
after all!

Willoughby was just about to tell
them his plan when Horatio interrupted.
"It's OK, I'm going to send a letter to
Santa, asking for help," he said. He held
up the bottle. "It's in here."

Horatio was about to toss it into the river when Starla gave a gasp. "Wait!" she said. "I've only just thought, the river is frozen, isn't it?"

"So?" Horatio shrugged.

"So the bottle won't *float*," Willoughby explained. And, of course, they were quite right. If Horatio threw his bottle over it would probably just smash on the ice.

"Oh, what now?" Horatio sighed, taking his letter out of the bottle. "Oh, I know!" he said. He folded the letter into a little paper aeroplane and launched it into the sky.

"Fly to Santa!" Horatio cried and, for a moment, it looked like it might.

Then the aeroplane's nose began to dip and it drifted down through the snow. Finally, it landed on the frozen river and Horatio heaved a heavy sigh.

"Hold on!" cried Riley, pointing his paw. *"Look!"*

A robin had spotted Horatio's letter and had snatched it up in his beak,

flying off with it through the sky. "Maybe he's taking it to Santa?" said Starla.

"Do you think so?" Horatio asked, his eyes growing wide.

"I do!" said Riley kindly. "Good job, Horatio!"

Willoughby smiled. "Right then!" he said. "Let me tell you my plan too!" So everyone listened carefully.

"Down the river, not far from here," Willoughby began, "I know a group of otters. They're really good swimmers, especially Oscar. Anyway, they could swim under the water and break the ice from underneath."

"So, they could clear a sort of pathway?" asked Starla.

"Yes," nodded Willoughby. "We just need a little bit of help to get us out of the creek. Then, when we get into deeper water, the ice shouldn't be so thick. And by then the boat will have picked up enough speed to break through it."

He suggested they walk along to find the otters. The snow was getting heavier by the minute so they set off right away.

They hadn't gone far when they spotted someone. Not an otter. Something much bigger.

"Oooh, look!" Starla gasped. "It's a *reindeer*!" They had seen lots of pictures of reindeers before, pulling Santa's sleigh but they'd never come across a *real* one. Reindeers were very shy indeed and didn't come out often.

The reindeer came trotting through the snow. His brown fur was as shiny as conkers and his deep dark eyes twinkled brightly. His antlers reminded Riley of curly branches!

"Hello!" said the reindeer in a friendly voice. "My name's Mistletoe, pleased to meet you!" He bowed his head and Willoughby smiled.

"Hello Mistletoe, I'm Willoughby White-Whiskers! And this is Starla, Horatio and Riley."

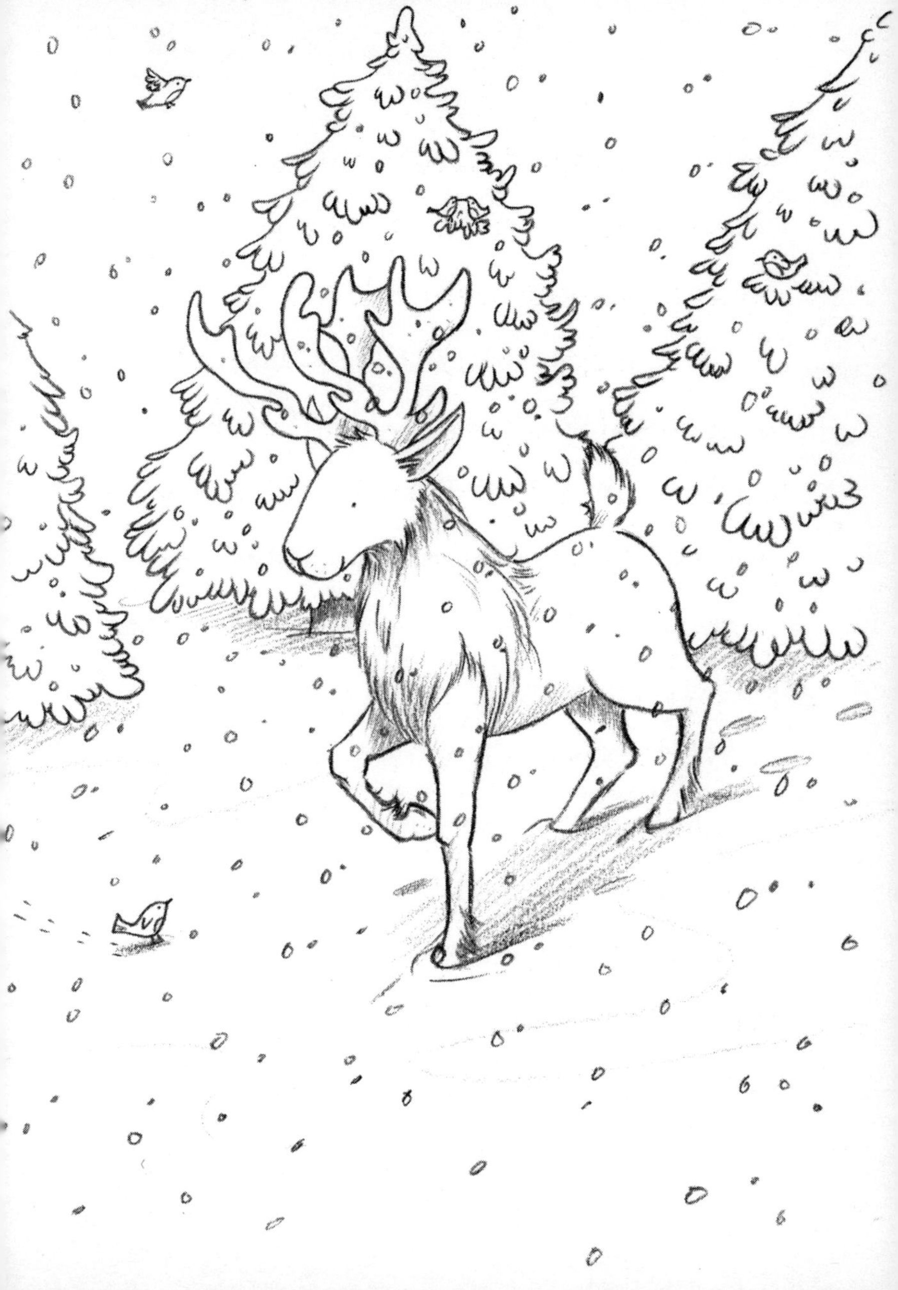

They smiled and Mistletoe bowed his head again.

"Is that your boat?" Mistletoe asked, looking behind Mr White-Whiskers to the *Kingfisher*.

"Yes," replied Willoughby. "But it's stuck in the ice. We're off to find my old friend, Oscar. The otters will help us out of here I'm sure!"

Mistletoe's smile suddenly dimmed. "The otters, you say? Ah, but they're gone. They went to visit their cousins last week and won't be back again until the New Year."

"Oh," said Willoughby, thinking hard.

"Hmmm, that *is* a shame." He'd have to think of something else and fast.

"Um," said Mistletoe, stepping closer. "Maybe I could help?"

"I *knew* it!" whispered Horatio to Riley and Starla. "I bet that robin took my letter to Santa and he sent one of his reindeers to help!" Horatio puffed out his chest proudly. "Clever me!"

Mr White-Whiskers looked at the reindeer. "Really?" he said. "You could help get us home?"

"I'd be happy to!" twinkled Mistletoe. "I could pull you all home in my sleigh. There's plenty of room for four, you know!"

"But what about our Christmas trees?" Starla asked. After they'd come all this way she didn't want to leave them behind.

"Well, my sleigh's big enough for those too!" Mistletoe nodded.

Willoughby's wise, old eyes shone brightly. "Thank you so much!" he said. "I'll just need to tie up the *Kingfisher* first and then we'll be ready to go."

Willoughby would come back and collect the boat when the ice had melted. He and Podrick Hare could sail up in the *Whirligig* then Podrick could sail one boat back while Willoughby sailed the other.

"I'll just get my sleigh then," Mistletoe smiled. "I hope you like fast rides!"

Chapter 5

The reindeer found his big sleigh and helped the friends load on the trees. Then they settled down among them on a soft, blue rug with the rest of Riley's mince pies and spiced ginger cordial.

"All safely aboard?" Mistletoe asked.

"All safely in!" called Willoughby.

"Yippee!" yelled Horatio, clapping his paws. "Let's go!"

Willoughby held the reins of the sleigh and Mistletoe trotted off.

"Wheee!" giggled Riley, Starla and Horatio. "Faster! Faster!"

They travelled through snowy meadows and fields as snowflakes swirled around them. Then on through woods and over soft, gentle hills.

All you could hear was the sound of hooves muffled by the thick snow and the happy squeals of Riley, Horatio and Starla.

They sped past a group of little snow hares bouncing around, throwing snowballs. Then a family of shivery robins huddled up on a fence.

As the friends whizzed along they pretended to be Santa, flying through the sky on Christmas Eve. Snowflakes stuck to Horatio's prickles, making him look like a funny snowball with short stumpy legs. "Ho! Ho! Ho!" he chuckled brightly. Tomorrow night the *real* Santa would be coming!

Finally, they picked up the path of the river and followed it towards home as the sky above their heads began to grow dark.

Little by little, the flat countryside began to get lumpier and bumpier as the moon and stars peeped down to light their way.

"Not much further to go now!" Willoughby said at last.

"I wonder what's for supper?" beamed Horatio.

When big, rolling hills surrounded them, they knew they were nearly home. Just as well, for now it was icy cold.

They arrived in Willow Valley just in time for supper, thanks to Mistletoe and his super-fast galloping!

Mimi-Rose heard the sound of hooves outside their cave-house and peeped through the window to see. "Mummy! Quick – there's a *reindeer*!" she cried.

They hurried outside as the sleigh stopped. "Who are you?" Mimi-Rose asked the reindeer.

"I'm Mistletoe!" he panted back.

"But, wait . . . I don't understand,"

said Riley's mum.

Willoughby explained everything as they unloaded Riley and his Christmas tree. "Now we must take the others home!" he said.

Before they set off, Riley's mum suggested that later Willoughby and Mistletoe came back to have supper with them.

Snow was now falling thickly and poor Mistletoe looked quite worn out. They couldn't expect him to travel back in the cold, dark night.

"You can sleep here tonight," said Riley's mum. "I'll pop a quilt by the fire for you and you can curl up on that."

"Oh, thank you," said Mistletoe with a smile. That sounded really nice!

Riley waved goodbye to Starla and Horatio as Mistletoe trotted them home. "See you tomorrow!" Riley called to his friends. Then suddenly he remembered – tomorrow was Christmas Eve! It was almost time for carols and roast chestnuts and *Santa*!

Riley pattered into his cosy cave-house, dragging his tree behind him. He left it in a corner of the kitchen, all ready to be decorated tomorrow.

While they were waiting for Mistletoe

to come back, Riley and his sister helped
their mum bake a delicious carrot
cake. It was cooling on the side when
Willoughby appeared with a *very* hungry
looking reindeer.

"Come in! Come in!" cried Riley's mum.
"I've made a lovely supper for us all!"

The meal began with a warming
soup – spiced parsnip and coriander.
It was *just* the thing they needed on a
frosty night!

Next, they tucked into a hearty sprout
pie with carrots, mashed potato and
gravy. (Even *sprouts* tasted yummy at
Christmas thought Riley!)

Pudding was their freshly baked carrot cake with a soft cream cheese frosting. Mistletoe wolfed it down and *even* managed seconds! "Mmm! This is the tastiest cake I've *ever* had!" he smiled.

After supper, Willoughby wandered home through the fields iced with snow as Mistletoe curled up in front of the glowing fire.

"Goodnight," said Riley and he pattered off to bed. Tomorrow he'd decorate his Christmas tree. What fun!

The next morning, Starla and Horatio came round to say goodbye to Mistletoe. "Thank you for bringing us home!" they said and Riley gave him a bag of mince pies for his journey.

They waved goodbye until he'd disappeared over the snow-covered hills. Now it was time to decorate their trees!

Starla led the way to her cave-house first. Her neat Christmas tree stood in a pot, her golden twinkle-cones all ready in a basket beside it.

Everyone helped her hang them on the branches, along with some silver baubles which sparkled like the pretty fireflies on the trees in Dingle Wood. "Oooh!" she smiled, gazing up at the branches. "It's lovely!"

Next, they went round to Horatio's house. Horatio's little brothers and sisters were all hiding in *his* tree. "Boo!" they giggled, popping out to surprise everyone.

Horatio found his huge star. Then he clambered up a step ladder and hung it at the top of his tall, wonky tree.

The star was *so* big and heavy that it bent the top branch down low. But Horatio didn't care a bit. "There!" he grinned, nodding his head. "Done!"

"Er, how about some *tinsel*?" Starla suggested as his tree still looked a little bare.

"Nah!" said Horatio brightly. "It's just right!"

He told them he liked big, bushy, wonky trees (which were a little bit bare). Besides, his tummy was calling for lunch. And lunch was *far* more important!

They went back to Riley's cave-house for lunch – pickles and bread and chutney and cheese. And a few more mince pies, of course!

After lunch, Riley's mum went up into the attic and brought down a big old box of decorations. She opened it up and they all peered in. "Wow!" cried Starla. "Look!"

There were candles and baubles and ribbons and tinsel. Everyone filled their paws and started decorating the tree.

Starla put on some pretty white candles. Then Mimi-Rose added some baubles. Riley's mum had made some striped candy canes. She brought them over on a little wooden tray and Horatio helped her hang them on the tree.

"What's happened to *that* one?" she said to Horatio. "It looks like someone's bitten it!"

Horatio shrugged, his cheeks turning pink but his mouth too full of candy cane to answer!

Finally, Riley hung on his paper chain and the tree was filled with white reindeers, reminding him of lots of little Mistletoes!

"It's the best tree *ever!*" squealed Mimi-Rose.

"Thanks," said Riley proudly.

After they had finished their decorating, Horatio and Starla helped Riley wrap presents then they played being Christmas elves in Riley's bedroom.

Before they knew it, it was time to

head to the village square for the carol singing. "You'll need your scarves and mittens tonight!" Riley's mum said. She lit them each a lantern to carry too.

They wrapped up warm and set off through the snow. Outside a sprinkle of tiny stars peeped down from the sky. It was going to be dark any minute now. Christmas Day would soon be here!

As they headed down the hill, more animals joined them. "I can't wait for my roast chestnuts," puffed Horatio. "I hope there'll be enough to go round!" Horatio liked carols but not *nearly* as much as roast chestnuts!

When they got to the village square, the big Christmas tree stood twinkling in the moonlight and the glow from shop windows made warm, golden puddles on the snow.

Animals were bustling about, buying their last Christmas presents, all in good spirits, and wishing each other a Merry Christmas.

Now everyone gathered under the Christmas tree beside a little mole orchestra, their trumpets and horns and flutes all at the ready!

Mumford Mole, Riley's teacher, would be playing his fiddle, and Willoughby stood at the front ready to conduct.

The moles always started with gentle carols and worked up to the more jolly ones later. And so they began with *Silent Night* and everyone sang in their sweetest voices.

The next carol was *Away in a Manger*. Riley's mum liked that one! Then they sang about donkeys and kings and shepherds with flocks that needed watching.

Soon everyone was singing at the tops of their voices and nobody cared if they got the tune wrong as they knew the roast chestnuts were coming!

Horatio was singing the loudest of all. "On the fifth day of Christmas the baker gave to me – five *ginger cakes*!"

"No, not ginger cakes!" Starla giggled. "Gold rings, Horatio. Gold rings!"

"Well, I would much rather have ginger cakes!" nodded Horatio.

After the carols, everyone nibbled on hot roast chestnuts around a crackling bonfire. There were toasted marshmallows too and gallons of delicious apple cordial!

Riley's friends talked about the presents they hoped they might get tomorrow. "I'd quite like some new books," said Starla. "And some knitting needles and wool."

"Well, I'm hoping for a *magic set*!" nodded Horatio.

"I want a walkie-talkie!" said a chatty red squirrel called Abigail Bright. "Then I can talk to Posy all day long!"

Posy Vole was Abigail's best friend but she didn't talk as much as Abigail. "What present would you like, Posy?" asked Starla.

"Um, earmuffs!" Posy replied.

"But then you won't hear Abigail *talking* to you!" giggled Riley.

Little Digby Mole was hoping for new spectacles as he'd lost his old ones a few weeks ago. And Bramble Bunny said he wanted a carrot-shaped kite!

As for Riley, he didn't mind what he got. Surprises were the best thing ever!

When the bonfire had finally burned low, it was time to go home and hang up their stockings.

"I've saved my last mince pie for Santa," Riley told his friends. "And Mum says she'll leave out some spiced ginger cordial too!"

As they wandered home under the stars Riley felt he would burst with excitement. Christmas Day was just one *tiny* sleep away. . .

Chapter 6

On Christmas morning Mimi-Rose shook Riley awake. "Riley! Riley!" she squeaked in his ear. *"It's Christmas!"*

Riley dived out of bed and they scurried off to wake up their mum. "Mum! Let's go and see if Santa's been!" cried Riley.

They whisked her out of bed and Riley found her slippers. Mimi-Rose was clutching a small bent wand and wore fairy wings over her Christmas elf pyjamas.

"I magic you wide awake!" she giggled, tapping the wand on her mum's head. Then they each took a paw and dragged her downstairs.

"Whoa!" grinned their mum. "Goodness me! Anyone would think it was Christmas!"

"It is! It is!" squeaked Mimi-Rose. "Come on!"

They hurried into the kitchen and Riley's eyes grew wide. The Christmas stockings hanging on the fireplace were overflowing with gifts. "And look!" cried Riley, pointing under the Christmas tree. "More presents!"

They took down their stockings
and dived in, eager to see what was
inside. There were nuts and seeds and
tangerines and rings of sweet, dried
apple. They nibbled and nibbled until
their mum said, "Save some for later!"

Next, Riley and Mimi-Rose began opening the pile of presents under the tree. They were wrapped in big shiny leaves and tied with bows of ivy. Some had clusters of berries on top. Others had sprigs of winter heather.

There were presents from Grandpa and some from their mum. Then Riley spotted a present for him from *Santa*.

"Look, Mum!" he beamed, fishing it out of the pile. He knelt down and popped it on his lap.

"Open it, Riley!" squealed Mimi-Rose excitedly.

Santa's gift was wrapped in handmade

paper and tied with a wide silver ribbon. On the top was a reindeer made out of fir cones. It had two currant eyes, curly twig antlers and its nose was a shiny red berry.

A gift tag hung from one of its antlers with a message written in gold. . .

To Riley,
Merry Christmas!
Love, Santa xxx
(PS. Open this gift with
Starla and Horatio!)

"I wonder what's inside?" cried Riley.
But he couldn't open it yet. Starla and
Horatio wouldn't be over until later.
He'd have to wait for them.

They carried on opening presents
as their porridge cooked on the stove.
Mimi-Rose got a mermaid book from
her mum with three paper mermaids to
dress in sparkly outfits.

Grandpa's gift to her was a mermaid
cave he'd carved from a hollowed-out
tree stump. It had tables and chairs and
little shell beds. And even a wardrobe to
hang all their beautiful clothes!

From Santa she got a huge tin of paints

and a very thick pad of paper. Now she'd be able to paint and paint, all year long!

Mimi-Rose gave her mum a bunny brooch she'd made out of pale pink pom-poms. "You can wear it every day!" she told her proudly.

"Wait! This will go with it!" Riley said. And he handed his mum a shiny stone necklace. He'd found the stones in his garden last autumn and had polished them until they shone.

Then he'd carefully glued them on to silky green ribbon with the biggest, shiniest stone in the middle. "I think the stones might be *jewels!*" he said.

"Me too!" beamed his mum. "They're so sparkly!"

Riley had made a jewel bracelet for his sister too, which made her squeal with joy. "It's my very best bracelet!" she cried and gave him a big Christmas hug to say thank you.

Grandpa's present to Riley was a smart wooden castle. It had a drawbridge that really went up and down, and turrets and winding staircases! There was also a trap door leading to a gloomy cellar.

Two brave wooden knights protected the castle, each with a shield and a shiny silver helmet. One wore a royal blue tabard and the other's was bright red.

They were clutching swords to fight off the dragon perched on the castle's tallest turret. He was blowing fire and looked *very* bad-tempered. "I think he needs a friend," said Mimi-Rose.

Riley's mum passed him a present

from her. "Thanks, Mum!" beamed Riley, his little black eyes twinkling.

He quickly slipped off the ivy ribbon and the shiny leaf wrapping fell open. Inside was a dark blue leather tube. Riley opened it and peeped inside. "A real map-making kit!" he cried. "Just wait till I show Horatio!"

There were rolled up scrolls of parchment and quills for drawing the maps. There were also three bottles of different coloured ink and some candles and stamps for making real wax seals.

It came with a book about famous explorers and how they made *their* maps. "This is brilliant!" Riley cried.

"Well, I know you want to be an explorer one day, so I thought you might like it!" said his mum.

"I do!" nodded Riley. "I really, really love it!"

Mimi-Rose gave him her present too. It was a little lion she'd made from yellow poms-poms. It had a lacy mane and two shiny bead eyes. Its teeth were rows of jagged card glued into a zigzaggy smile. "Now Lionel can make friends with your grumpy old dragon!" Mimi-Rose smiled.

"Good idea!" giggled Riley. "Thanks!"

After breakfast, they played with their new toys. Riley kept glancing at Santa's present, wondering what it might be. Then, just before lunch, Starla and Horatio arrived.

Horatio had been given the magic set

he'd really wanted for Christmas. He swished in wearing a magician's hat and starry cape to match.

"I've even got a *wand*!" he cried, swishing it wildly through the air. As he did, a big bunch of flowers popped down from under his hat.

"Ooops!" grinned Horatio, peeping through the petals. "That wasn't meant to happen! I think I might need a little bit more practice. . ."

Starla had a new pair of roller skates. She wobbled around the Christmas tree and everybody clapped. Then Riley showed them Santa's wrapped up gift.

"Oh, *we've* each got one of those!" cried Starla, skating to her basket and taking hers out. "And ours say we should open them together too!"

Horatio whisked his out from under his hat but a big clump of daisies sprang out too.

"Let's open them in my bedroom!" grinned Riley. "Come on!"

Starla took off her skates and they hurried upstairs. They all knelt down on Riley's rug and then, on the count of three, opened their presents together. . .

"Wow!" said Riley.

"Oooh!" gasped Starla.

"Cor!" cried Horatio. *"Look!"*

Santa had given them each a snow-globe. They were filled with water and tiny white snowflakes that swirled and tumbled down.

Inside Horatio's was a jolly Santa riding on a sleigh. Reindeers were pulling it through the moonlit sky. The one at the front looked *just* like the reindeer who had galloped them home through the snow. "I think this one is Mistletoe!" cried Horatio.

Starla's snow-globe had a Christmas tree inside. It looked *exactly* like the one in Dingle Wood with the beautiful fireflies that twinkled on its branches. On the top was the shiniest star she'd ever seen. "I'll treasure it forever!" she beamed.

Inside Riley's snow-globe three friends were playing in the snow. There was a little brown mouse, a smiley badger and a roly-poly hedgehog. "Wait a minute!"

Riley cried. "They're *us!*"

This snow-globe would live on Riley's bedside table *all year long*, reminding him of the snowy day they had spent together. One snowy day he would never, *ever* forget.

Visit

all year round!

WILLOW VALLEY

The Big Bike Race
Tracey Corderoy

"I wish
I lived in
Willow Valley!"
Philippa
Forrester

WILLOW VALLEY

Hide and Seek
Tracey Corderoy

"I wish
I lived in
Willow Valley!"
Philippa
Forrester

Look out for
a very special summer story
COMING SOON!